Wynken, Blynken, and Nod

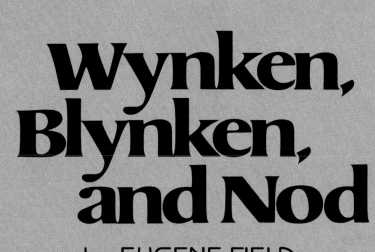

Wynken, Blynken, and Nod

by EUGENE FIELD

illustrated by SUSAN JEFFERS

E. P. DUTTON · NEW YORK

for Nanny and Auntie Lor
with love

"Wynken, Blynken, and Nod," a poem by Eugene Field

Illustrations copyright © 1982 by Susan Jeffers

Library of Congress Cataloging in Publication Data
Field, Eugene, 1850–1895.   Wynken, Blynken, and Nod.
Summary: In this bedtime poem, three fishermen in a
wooden shoe catch stars in their nets of silver and gold.
1. Children's poetry, American. [1. American poetry]
I. Jeffers, Susan, ill.   II. Title.
PS1667.W8   1982   811'.4   82-2434
ISBN 0-525-44022-4   AACR2

Published in the United States by E. P. Dutton, Inc.,
2 Park Avenue, New York, N.Y. 10016

Published simultaneously in Canada by Clarke,
Irwin & Company Limited, Toronto and Vancouver

Editor: Ann Durell   Designer: Riki Levinson

Printed and bound in Hong Kong
by South China Printing Co.
First Edition   10 9 8 7 6 5 4 3 2 1

Wynken, Blynken, and Nod one night
Sailed off in a wooden shoe—

Sailed on a river of crystal light,
Into a sea of dew.

"Where are you going, and what do you wish?"
The old moon asked the three.

"We have come to fish for the herring fish
That live in this beautiful sea.

Nets of silver and gold have we!"
Said Wynken, Blynken, and Nod.

The old moon laughed and sang a song
As they rocked in the wooden shoe,

And the wind that sped them all night long
Ruffled the waves of dew.

The little stars were the herring fish
That lived in that beautiful sea.

"Now cast your nets wherever you wish—
    Never afeard are we!"
So cried the stars to the fishermen three:
    Wynken, Blynken, and Nod.

All night long their nets they threw
    To the stars in the twinkling foam.

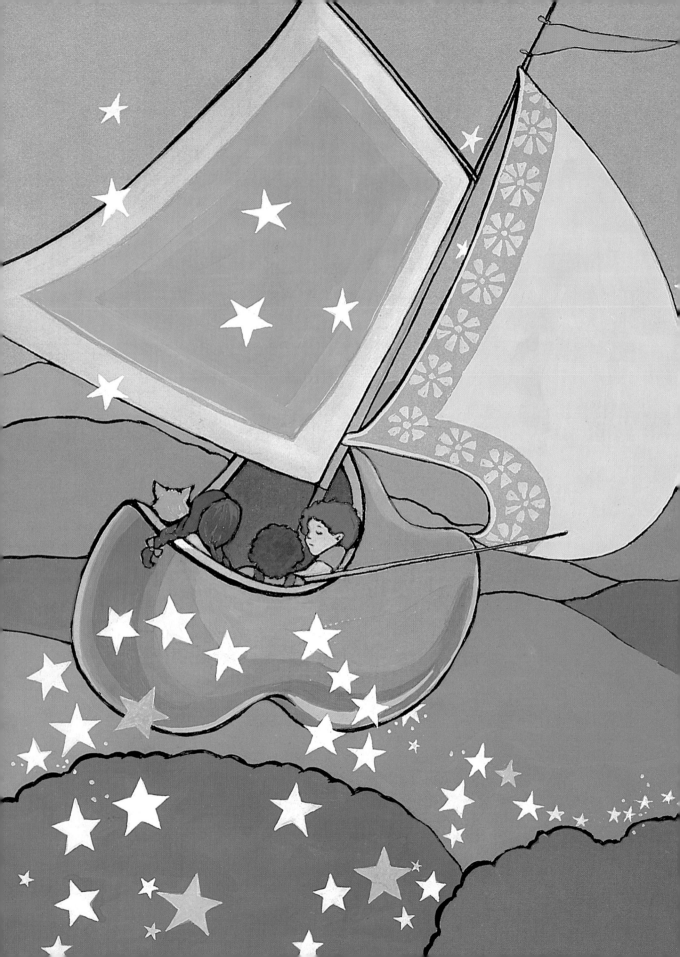

Then down from the skies came the wooden shoe,
  Bringing the fishermen home.

'Twas all so pretty a sail, it seemed
      As if it could not be;
And some folks thought 'twas a dream they'd dreamed
      Of sailing that beautiful sea.

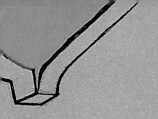

But I shall name you the fishermen three:
　　Wynken, Blynken, and Nod.

Wynken and Blynken are two little eyes,
　　And Nod is a little head,
And the wooden shoe that sailed the skies
　　Is a wee one's trundle bed.

So shut your eyes while Daddy sings
Of wonderful sights that be,
And you shall see the beautiful things
As you rock on the misty sea

Where the old shoe rocked the fishermen three:
Wynken, Blynken, and Nod.